To NHS and family, thank you for all your support in life!

Part of the income generated from the sale of this book will be donated straight to the NHS as a token of our gratitude.

CONTENTS

Part One, The Grammar Grandma

Chapter 1- Time for School

Chapter 2- The Arrival at Cansher Primary School

Chapter 3- The Nasty Attack of Greedy Gotham

Chapter 4- Lovebirds

Chapter 5- Time for Class

Chapter 6- Meanwhile...

Chapter 7- Let Me Tell You All About It (1)

Chapter 8- Back to The Story

Chapter 9- Let Me Tell You All About It (2)

Chapter 10- Back to The Story (again)

Chapter 11- The Crazy Chase

Chapter 12- A sticky situation

Chapter 13- Let Me Tell You All About It (3)

Chapter 14- Back to the story (again)

Chapter 15- Food Fight Business

Chapter 16- Finally!

Part Two, The Maths Mech

Chapter 17- What a Mess

Chapter 18- The Massive Catastrophe

Chapter 19- Oh No

Chapter 20- Trouble

Chapter 21- The perspectives of the other kids

Chapter 22- Hometime

Chapter 23- The end is near

Chapter 24- The journey back

Once upon a time lived a smart boy - wait, wait, wait! I haven't introduced myself properly yet. My name is Anil Buyukadam. When you see this icon around speech -, it means that I am pausing the story, normally to say something that I want to say, ok carry on now -, his name was Marvellous Mester and he lived on Chesterseet Avenue. Little did he know, a thrilling plethora of adventures was heading straight for him, right now. you on the edge of your seat yet? -

Part One - The Grammar Grandma

Chapter 1- Time for School

One day was a normal day, Mester thought to himself. - read till the end to find out that this was a rollercoaster of a ride for Mester and his funny friends. They learnt new things about the subject grammar or shall I say grrrrrrammar! – His friends were just at the end of the alley, walking to school to learn new things. "Hi," Mester shouted cheerfully to his friends, at the top of his lungs. His friends enthusiastically replied, "Hi!" Mester marched towards his friends, as proud as a perfect boy. His friends glared at him, suspiciously. "Is anything wrong," questioned Harry, puzzled. He replied merrily, "No." Surely, his friends thought something peculiar was going to lurk out of this typical day, or shall I say, mysterious day. They just forgot about it and carried on with their ordinary lives. They finally arrived at their school, this was also peculiar because of the name, Cansher Primary School. This day was getting more and more tense, just saying.

Chapter 2- The Arrival at Cansher Primary School

When they went inside, as usual, the school bully, Greedy Gotham as we called him, lurked around the school terrorising the school, stealing snacks. That's why we call him greedy. When he hovered past us, the tension was building, just seeing that mouthful of chocolate, most of which was dripping down his mouth onto his chin and departing his skin. - You scared yet? Well it will get scarier in a bit when Marvellous Mester stands up to the bully. Mester is rather skinny, just saying if you want to put it that way. – When he slithered past us, as slow as a sloth, he exchanged a glare, a nasty and dirty one I'd say.

Chapter 3- The Nasty Attack of Greedy Gotham

Blood rapidly travelled through our veins as he seized a tiny kid that was minding his business. "OI, GIVE ME A TASTY BAR OF CHOCOLATE OR I WILL TURN YOU INTO OBLIVION, screeched the school bully. It was time for Mester's move, or shall I say, scary fail. "Put him down or ELSE, scrooched Mester, as scared as a soft cat. "OR ELSE WHAT?!" "Here we go again," sighed Harry and Alfie. The barbaric bully let go of him and then grabbed Mester. "Help," squealed Mester. At least he was miraculous for saving the kid's life from the bully. Just then, a crowd of anxious children gathered round this greedy bully, all shivering. "OI, YOU LOT, SCRAM OR ELSE I WILL TURN YOU ALL INTO MASHED POTATOES," retorted Greedy Gotham. His rather loud voice pierced the air like scissors cutting through thin paper.

Ralph then came in. He said in a crisp, clear voice, "Leave my friend ALONE!" - He is rather fierce I'd say – "Yeah, leave him alone," echoed George. This started a colossal chant that went into a series of words that shouted, "Leave him alone, leave him alone." "OK, ok, I will leave him alone." When he said these words monstrously, he had a trick up his sleeve. Mester was then dropped to the floor like he was useless.

When this happened, Greedy Gotham was laughing boisterously. - This is getting to the main part of the story as I speak. –

Chapter 4- Lovebirds

"Are you ok?" whispered Jane, the head girl for being the smartest girl. "Y..Y..Yes T..T.. Thank Y..Y..You," stammered Mester. Jane and Mester were lovebirds because they were both the smartest. "No problem," said Jane, gleefully. "I act like this as well, so you are not alone." Mester's heart skipped a beat. It seemed like he might as well faint. "Err, I will stay out of this so enjoy your love fest," trembled Jessica, one of the pupils that witnessed this rather awkward sight. Jake came in and asked, "What is going on here?" – Ok enough with the chit-chatting, just get to the main part of the story- "Nothing so stay out of it," roared Ralph. Jake, you know, is a rather nosey kid in Cansher Primary.

Most of the girls, like Val, Alesha and Alyssa came rushing through to see if Mester was all right. Following this, a torpedo of children also came zooming past to check if he was all right. Mester got up to his knees once the bully had departed the gargantuan crowd. Mester then carried on journeying to his grammar class. "GRAMMAR CLASS," shouted the rather overweight grammar teacher.

"Oooh, I love grammar," said Mester restlessly. When they took off for their big adventure, or shall I say, off to see the grammar grandma, they were heading for the class. Ring! Ring! Ring! "Time for class," he thought.

Chapter 5- Time for Class

Everyone was in class apart from The Fashion Girl. At least that's what we called her. "Alfie." "Here." "Jane." "Here I am, the most gracious teacher in the world." Everyone started roaring with laughter. - I bet you know why this event is hard to not gossip about. - "Oh, thank you Jane, that's really kind of you," said the grammar teacher, blushing. Her voice was crisp, clean, which did not happen very often. "Anyways, Jester."

"Here," said Jester. Someone decided to go over the top and say something silly. "DAMM FEELS GOOD TO BE A GANGSTER," shouted Val in an awkward tone. The class screeched with laughter. This was so funny that some of the boys' cheeks went red as they scrooched with this amount of laughter. "SILENCE!" The grammar teacher's voice cut through the air like thin paper. - Sorry, I might use some of my similes over and over in this particular story. :)

Chapter 6- Meanwhile...

At this moment, an angry mob of children were forming; because of this, the school was being terrorised. This started from Greedy Gotham stealing everyone's snacks so they decided to get revenge on him, a perfect comeback. When the mob approached its victim, it began to make the plot of the scene. "OI, COME HERE YOU GREEDY, FAT PIG," shouted the mob, which was still forming as we speak. They were approaching

Reception, the weirdest class in the even weirder school. - This class was referred to as 'The Children Ruling Over Teachers' class. Reason why? Well, let me tell you all about it.

Chapter 7- Let Me Tell You All About It (1)

Basically, Reception just become the teachers and the teachers become their pupils along with many teddies. Who knows what caused this drama? Actually, before you and your friends sigh, I know why. So, once upon a time, lived a creature called Lexer. She controlled the teachers to be children forever or else. Also, she then told the receptions that they could control the teachers.

That's basically it. You and your friends can sigh now. –

Chapter 8- Back to The Story

Ok, so where were we. Ah. There we go. "OR ELSE," said the scary barricade of children. - Sorry, but we have to get used to this rather loud conversation. - "OR ELSE WHAT," said Greedy Gotham, grasping what he had said in not the too distant past. "OR ELSE WE WILL TURN YOU INTO DUST, YOU OVERWEIGHT CAT!" - Ok, this is not a good time right now to be arguing - "ACTUALLY, I WILL TURN YOU ALL INTO PRAWNS," said Greedy Gotham, bravely. The barricade divided into all the pupils that formed this barricade. All the pupils shivered and trembled, of course, apart from Greedy Gotham. "We are sorry and we will go back to our classroom in an orderly fashion," shivered Usher, the only person to have a name starting with a 'U'. Gotham's face turned from a prawny pale to a blazing red. "I WILL CATCH YOU AND OBLIVERATE YOU INTO MICROSCOPIC PIECES," shouted Gotham, his mouth still covered in chocolate. "Wow, he actually knows the word, microscopic," said Antony, surprised and astonished. "Now to RUN!" The crowd retreated from the fat bully. - I forgot to mention that there are more bullies in the school, like Fat Figo and Overweight Oscar. These are some of the cruel bullies at school. They all like to fight at a place called the Bully Brawl. Let me tell you all about it.

Chapter 9- Let Me Tell You All About It (2)

Once upon a time, lived a hideous bully named Boasting Brad. Once, he met up with his friends, who were also bullies. He said, "I can build anything I want." His friends looked at him, doing the 'We know you are boasting' face. He then looked at them angrily and said, "I will build a bully brawl so we can call hang out, OK?" "Stop lying, you cannot even place a brick, you fool," shouted one of the bullies, brutally. All the bullies in the school started roaring with the amount of laughter contaminated inside them. Even one of the bullies was playing Fortnite on his phone, how cheeky! Boasting Brad then got so tempered that he viciously snatched the bully and carried him in the air. He then started the weirdest auction to ever live. "Rude bully for sale, let's start with £150," shouted Boasting Brad. "£200," screamed Brutal Bendy.

"Rude bully going for £200 to Brutal Bendy," said Boasting Brad. "£500!" Rude bully going for £500 to Vile Vex in 10, 9, 8, 7, 6, 5, 4, 3, 2, 1, and ...." "£1000 pounds," screeched Merciless Max. "Sold!" "YOU WILL REGRET THIS," shouted the bully. "Ok, now to build this bully brawl," he thought to himself. - 2000 years later.... - "Done," he said, as proudly as a soldier. And that's how a bully brawl appeared. - Ok, one or two more things I would like to add.

First and foremost, Boasting Brad usually just lies to get everyone's attention, even the ones playing on their phone. He always and I mean ALWAYS wants to be at the centre of attention because he is normally separated from people, which caused him to feel lonely and isolated from the rest of the world. No wonder he is such a show off! Oh, wait, then how do I know this when I used the words 'No wonder' at the sentence before?

Well, guess it's a mystery in history. Nice, now I rhymed two words. I really am smart. Ok, before we get back to the story let's think of a word that rhymes with rhyme. Don't read on until you thought of one, unless you want to skip this part. (Ding!) Ok, I thought of the word, chime, time, crime, and mime. How about you? If you thought of the words shrine or vine, you were close.

There are more, still so you can try to find all of them if you really want to. Ok, back to the story.

Chapter 10- Back to The Story (again)

Ok, where were we? Ah, yes, there we were. "I WILL TURN YOU INTO PIE," hissed Greedy Gotham, still enraged with the anger that was inside him, lurking about and bringing more despair and greed to him. The crowd, as I said, ran away like they were a flight of mice, fleeing away from Greedy Gotham, a smart and decisive move. "YOU CAN RUN BUT YOU CAN'T HIDE," he shouted.

Chapter 11- The Crazy Chase

"RUN, he's still on our tail. Don't just stop now, Ashley and Zee," screamed Renny. At her expectations, Joy would have still been running. And she was inaccurate. Joy was taking a breather because he has been running for a while now about a few miles. "Come on, the bully is closing in on us!" And he was. Every second he was nearing in on everyone. People were shrieking with horror as he stumbled to try and grab people hastily.

Chapter 12- A sticky situation

"How RUDE to interrupt me by some bickering and laughter," shouted the grammar teacher in a fiery and waspish voice. "Ok, let's forget this just ever happened.

She paused to breathe and then resumed talking. "Mina," she said in a raspy voice. "Of course," she murmured. "Of course, she is always late, LATE!" Some of the students gasped reacting to the high frequency volume of her very loud shouting. - This is why I said at the beginning, 'grrrrrrammar'. - This was so loud that her high-pitched shouting appeared as, let's say, squeaky-shouting. The school rumpled like an insecure pile of mud.

This felt like a series of aftershocks before she shouted, which was the part when the earthquake-like force began. This was so loud that everyone was muted after the devasting voice sliced through the air. Mina (aka, the Fashion Girl) burst through the antique wooden doors as the other pupils were experiencing a lion-like roar the teacher managed to create with her vocal cords. "You're late," said one of the pupils.

The teacher just, well, sighed. "Please just go to your desk and sit down and let's get on with this, shall we," sighed the grammar teacher. "Ugh, fine like whatever," groaned Mina. The school shook again. This time it was Farting Freddy. Sounds stinky, right? Everyone held their breath as the gas cloud stormed through the classroom and departed through the glass-paned window.

"Great, now I'm smelly," said Mina, acting like she was the only important one in the classroom. Once the gas cloud left the room, it entered the secret clubhouse where the boss of kids lived. Let me tell you all about it.

Chapter 13- Let Me Tell You All About It (3)

One day, a cool kid dared to enter the school grounds, although he was banned from Cansher Primary School. All the kids loved him, like the cool kid was a celebrity or a successful kid. Why was he not allowed on the school grounds? It was because he was too famously known for his willing attitude to learning, which made him that successful. So he was given a secret clubhouse and also crowned head boy.

I bet Mester would love that if he accomplished it. Well, Jane has accomplished head girl but head kid went to the cool kid. The teachers couldn't resist but give the title to him. Until it came to last year. Then, they gave the title to Mester. He was overjoyed being told this wondrous news. But the cool kid was now sad and lonely. He was still a bit happy because he was crowned the longest person to be head boy in Cansher history.

Chapter 14- Back to The Story (again)

Everyone gasped as the stinkbomb entered the secret clubhouse. Even the teacher was dazed to witness such a disgraceful sight. "Peweeee," replied the cool kid. "Where did THAT come from," shouted the cool kid. "The causer replied. "Oh, I'm soooo sorry master," said Farting Freddy, hoping he would forgive him.

Well, his hopes turned out to be a downer. "I will NOT forgive you!" Farting Freddy wailed as he failed to make the cool kid forgive him. The cool kid then just sighed and went back to the clubhouse. "As I was trying to say but couldn't after all this clatter, Ofsted are coming to inspect the school in a few weeks," said the grammar teacher, calmly. She then continued talking. "As you all know, for the past history of our school, we have never been rated an outstanding.

We have mostly been rated a…a….an," trembled the grammar teacher. "an….an…inadequate," she stormed. - Just to let you know, the grammar teacher hates and I mean HATES the word ok. She thinks it's not enough to actually pursue something. - "We need to upper our game if we want to beat Ashley CE Primary School." "Ok," said the class, most of which was yawning. - 3 hours later – Once it was lunch time, all the kids gathered up to the canteen to get some food for them to eat. "OI, GIVE ME YOUR CHIPS AND BURGER OR YOU WILL BE MY CHIPS AND BURGER!" Gotham shouted so loud which caused the city to suddenly shake. - I would classify Greedy Gotham as a piece of monstrosity! How about you? - The kid said in a squeaky tone, "No." Greedy Gotham was now infuriated and then clutched the kid and waved him in the air. Everyone started booing at the bully until he then tossed the kid onto the marble floor that was once polished to sparkle. Once Greedy Gotham chucked him onto the floor, he grabbed some food and started plunging it at other kids. "FOOD FIGHT," cawed one of the kids, bursting the words out of his mouth. Everyone obeyed and started launching food at each other. This caused the cafeteria to look all grubby, like a pig sty. Because Mester disapproved of this, he exited the cafeteria and eventually disembarked at the classroom.

When Mester entered, he exchanged glances with the grammar teacher. "Why are you down in the dumps, Mester," asked the grammar teacher politely. "It's just that..." Mester then took a deep breath before he carried on. "It's just that every one aren't making a change to make this school successful." The grammar teacher gave him an expression that said, "I know Mester, I know." Suddenly, Jane interrupted by barging into the classroom.

"Miss, everyone is having a food fight in the canteen!" The grammar teacher turned around to sort out this alarming situation. "Thanks for notifying me Jane," gleed the grammar teacher. - Since I'm having to use the term, 'the grammar teacher,' I will reveal her name. She is called Elize. Now, let's carry on with the story, shall we? - "I will now proceed to the canteen to deal with this heck of a mess.

Chapter 15- Food Fight Business

When Elize stormed into the canteen like a wild trooper, she startled everyone with just the spicy look on her face. Every single pupil, apart from Gotham, rushed to their seats like soldiers, obeying the boss's command. "GOTHAM!" "Yes Miss," replied Greedy Gotham. "KEEP YOUR HANDS TO YOURSELF," she snorted. - Elize wasn't happy right now. I wouldn't even use the term, angry.

I'd use the term, steaming. - "Yes, Miss," meowed Gotham. Elize then took a sigh to loosen her rage. "Well, the teacher was very malicious," whispered Ralph. He was chatting to Harry while the canteen was bustling with noise. "And also, stop catapulting food at each other; it's disrespectful," Elize requested. Everyone listened and stopped throwing food so a future complaint about this won't come out of Elize's mouth.

"Yes, Miss Elize," replied the pupils. "Thank you everybody," sighed Elize. Once she left, the noise stood to a halt and everything remained silent.

Chapter 16- Finally!

"Finally, some peace and quiet," she murmured to herself as she strode gently through the narrow corridors of the gargantuan school. "Thanks," said Mester and Jane as Miss Elize glided into the room like an agile butterfly speeding through the polished hallways and into the spacious classroom. "Just doing my duty," she countered. Elize felt as proud as a woman fulfilling her task set by a proper student rather than a kid. This actually happened. She compled a task set by a pupil. Ok, back to the story. They all smirked at each other, just for fun. "You know Miss Elize," blushed Mester. "Yes?" "You feel like a grandma to me." Jane and Elize sobbed with happy tears. "You know, that's one of the nicest things a student has ever said to me," teared Miss Elize merrily. Ring! Ring! The bell went and that signalled end of lunch time. "Ok, cautiously walk to your next class," she announced to Mester and Jane.

Part Two, The Maths Mech

Chapter 17- What a Mess

They arrived at their destination, the maths class, where big numbers, equations, square roots, and algebra, came in. That was only the starters. Do you know why this sounds so complex? It's because a mech, as we call it, teaches us. Get distracted and then get bopped on the head with a ruler. Trust me, you don't want to be in this situation.

The mech was called M.A.T.H which is an acronym for Mechanical Artificial Technological Highbrow. Also, the reason the chapter is called 'What a Mess' is because the robot was out of control. For some reason, it wasn't functioning properly. Maybe the software was clogged with water from the day it decided to use glass bottles filled with water when it was teaching pupils fractions while we were in grammar class. Who knows?

All we know is that it's getting out of control! "System shuting down." As the robot said the next word, it's voice went deeper and deeper until it collapsed onto the floor. The children stepped back in fright as they saw the ironic-like robot disintergrate.

Chapter 18- The Massive Catastrophe

"Who will teach us now," questioned Ashley. "Who cares," retaliated Mina, blowing chewing gum and yanking it from her mouth and sticking it under the wooden, sturdy table. "Mina, you are not allowed to have gum in the school premises," bursted out Mester. "What, then I can't eat food!" Mina's squad roared at Mester.

"Errr, I don't think that you should have put it that way," interrupted Jane. "Because they are all roaring at you in laughter." Mester just then looked down at his shoes. This conversation caused everyone to quarrel over at each other because there was no teacher/robot teacher to tell the kids to pipe down.

Chapter 19- Oh No!

While everyone was squabbling at each other, Mester and Jane heard the head teacher thudding his feet as he marched through the thin corridors all the way to class 5B, the class we are in right now. Mester and Jane rushed to their seats as the rest of the class ignored the troll-like footsteps. The head teacher's name was Mr Sanchez and he was very strict as of the school rules. His favourite student was, well actually, he had three favourites, Mester, Jane and the cool kid. He would transform from a tempestuous troll to a benevolent butterfly once he just gets a glimpse of one of them. Stomp! Stomp! Stomp! His eerie footsteps got louder and louder until the whole school was notified that he was walking. Yes, even the Reception class heard his footsteps fade into abyss as he stormed past them. All the teachers gulped as they heard him march past them. Even the robots were anxious that he might do any harm to them. Most of Year 5 were scared of him. Only Mester and Jane weren't scared of him for a reason. And that reason was because he liked them. So they liked him back. Mr Sanchez, at his raging state, slammed the doors open as he entered class 5B. "What in the law's name is going on," shouted Mr Sanchez. Everyone walked to their seats to reveal the corrupted robot that fell out of it's place. "Woah, that robot took some serious damage in the doing of this lesson! Who is responsible for this valuable robot malfunctioning?" "Not me," echoed the whole class. "Of course, typical children," replied Mr Sanchez. "No seriously, it wasn't us," exclaimed Mester. "Then who was it then?" "It collapsed," replied Mester. "How?" "Ask the other Year Fives." So Mr Sanchez strode to 5A where the grammar teacher was. "Have you any idea how the robot failed to function?"

"Ask the students, Mr Sanchez," replied Miss Elize in a well mannered way. "Errrr you, do you know how the robot broke?" "The robot was teaching us percentages by using these plastic containers," confirmed one of the kids. "He then spilt one of the containers and as that happened, the water flowed towards the robot, entering it once the water left the table." "Thank you for clarifying," replied Mr Sanchez.

He then left class 5A, only to go back to class 5B. Mr Sanchez then slammed open the doors, once again to march into class 5B. "Alright, guess I will be your substitute teacher for today." Mina groaned because she knew that Mr Sanchez would give her detention first thing. "DETENTION!" Mina saw this coming as she walked out of the room, her head drooping at the floor.

Mina left the class, as she planned, only to sneak to the vending machines. The school cleaner just turned around the bend to walk to the cafeteria. The cleaner took a glance at Mina when he shouted, "You're meant to be in class, missy!" Mina huffed and retorted, "Mind your own business!"

Chapter 20- Trouble

"Don't you DARE talk back to an adult like that! Where's your teacher?" "Not telling you." While the two squabbled, Mr Sanchez was thoroughly listening. "Hmm, okay, this missy needs to be taught some manners! He then zoomed out of the class, his back trembling. "But wait," said Max. Mr Sanchez stomped out of the class and bolted in a violent way towards the school cleaner and Mina.

"What is this nonsense about?" "Mina's not meant to be here!" "MINA! GET IN CLASS NOW! AND SIT IN THE CORNER!" Mina groans, "Ugh." "Typical Mina," sighed Mr Sanchez. He then grabbed and shook her hand whilst pulling her back. "But I don't want to learn," Mina wailed. "TOUGH!" Mr Sanchez was back to his moody, grumpy self. Once Mr Sanchez dragged Mina through the hallway back to the classroom, Mina was forced to sit on the floor in the corner of the class. "Now as I was saying, we will be doing maths," said Mr Sanchez. Mester shook his hand up. "Yes?" "What topic are we going to be focusing on?" "Oh yes thanks for reminding me. We will be learning about lattice multiplacation. Jane raised her hand up. "Yep?" "What exactly is lattice multiplacation?" "I was just getting to that bit, Jane." "Oh." "So lattice multiplacation is a grid that looks like this.

Mr Sanchez drew a grid on the board looking like a rectangle split into six squares in a three by two formation. There were also diagonal lines starting from the top right going down to the bottom left of the squares, dividing the squares into two triangles per square. The diagonal lines also go one more to the bottom left once they come off the grid. That seperates the answers, but we will get to that bit in a second.

"So we will be doing 647x49. So we put the 6 for six hundred above the square that is on the coordinates (2,1). Next, we put the 4 for forty above the square that is on the coordinates (2,2). After that, we put the 7 for seven over the square that is on the coordinates (2,3)." Alli put his hand up. "Yes?" "So now have you put the number 647 in the grid?" "Well not in the grid but on top of the grid. But I could see where you was going Alli. Well done!" "Thank you!"

"You're welcome. Ok, as I was talking about, we've inserted the number 647 so now we have to put the number 49. We put the 4 for forty in the right hand side of the square that is on the coordinates (2,3). Lastly for this part, we put the 9 for nine in the right hand side of the square that is on the coordinates (1,3). Now, we have put the numbers 647 and 49 outside of the grid. Now we have to times the numbers.

Lets start with 6 from the top times 4 from the side. So we write the answer in the box in the coordinates (2,1) because if 6 made a line down and 4 made a line across, they would meet at that box. So we write the answer in that box. We write the tens answer in the left triange and we write the ones answer in the right triangle. 6x4=24 so we write the two in the left triangle and we write the four in the right triangle in the box. And we do the same for the other numbers. So the answer to 647x49 would be 31,703. Get it?" "Yes, replied the class. "No, creaked Mina. "BECAUSE CLEARLY, YOU WEREN'T LISTENING!" "I was," fibbed Mina. "I don't trust you from all them times you lied to me. And you are certainly not LOYAL!" Mina shed into tears, thinking about all the times everyone hated her. Mina was just a lonely girl that just wanted some friends, some reliability and some fun. This is why she was mean.

The world was cruel to her, so she had no choice but to be dreadful. She done this because if she doesn't get treated nicely, she wouldn't treat others nicely. - No wonder she always misbehaved while she was in class. – "STOP CRYING AND ACT LIKE A BEHAVED CHILD, WILL YOU," Mr Sanchez tormented. Mina then burst into more tears, sounding like a baby that wants it's teddy bear back. Some of the bullies burst into tears of laughter as they witnessed a ten year old cry like a one year old. – How impolite and rude! – "OI! STOP LAUGHING OR YOU WILL BE IN THIS STATE TOO!" CHILD, WILL YOU," Mr Sanchez tormented. Mina then burst into more tears, sounding like a baby that wants it's teddy bear back. Some of the bullies burst into tears of laughter as they witnessed a ten year old cry like a one year old.

How impolite and rude! – The laughter stood to a halt as Mr Sanchez hollered these words, "OI! STOP LAUGHING OR YOU WILL BE IN THIS STATE TOO!" "Yes Mr Sanchez, Greedy Gotham whizzed, as scared as a mouse. "That's better," said Mr Sancheez, calmly. Mina was still wailing in the corner of the classroom and nobody tried to make her feel better, apart from Usher, who just elegantly walked to Mina.

"AND WHAT DO YOU THINK YOU'RE DOING," Mr Sanchez burst out. "Sorry, I was just going to Mina to try and cheer her up," Usher quaked. Mina then gazed up at Usher, hoping to be making friends with her. "Fine, just make her stop crying, will you?" – Since we have been talking about this chapter, lets see what the others were doing.

Chapter 21- The perspectives of the other kids

While Class 5B were trying to learn about lattice multiplacation but because of Mina, the class were being delayed, Class 5A were learning about, you guessed it, grammar. Miss Elize was teaching the class about the suffix -ing and -ed. Now lets turn the story over to this class. "So, can you give me an example of a word that ends with an -ing?" "Umm, crashing," replied Pete. "Thank you Pete, now can I have a word that ends with the suffix, -ed from somebody else?" – Just to notify you, this class is well more behaved than group 5A, apart from Mester and Jane, of course. Also, not to confuse you but Mester's class are in group 5A but they are in class 5B. So earlier, they were in class 5A with MIss Elize but now group 5B is in class 5A. Now back to the story. – "Alexandra, can you please say a word that ends in the suffix -ed," queried Miss Elize.

"Does stampeded end with -ed?" "Well done Alexandra," said Miss Elize gleefully. "Yay," cheered Alexandra joyfully. "Now we have seen an example of a word ending in -ing and -ed, lets give out the sheets; who wants to volunteer giving out the papers with me?" "Me," said Jones, the person who is esteemed to help people anytime, anywhere. "Ok, you can help me hand out the sheets," countered Miss Elize. Jones then rose out of his seat, as neatly as a narwhal, to go and collect the sheets that he's going to give out. "Thanks for helping out, by the way," said Miss Elize. When he gave out the sheets, Miss Elize read, "Write ten words that ends with -ed and five words that ends in -ing. Shall we start?" "Ok," replied the class. Once the children finished their learning, and I'm talking about all of the classes, it was time to go home.

Chapter 22- Hometime

"Chop chop everybody, it's hometime." The class sighed, "Already? Can't we learn more?" "I am sorry class, but it's three o' clock, so you have to go home," replied Miss Elize, regrettably. "So can all of you please get your stuff and wait by the door?" The kids obeyed and got their stuff and lined up at the door, ready to be called out for when their parents arrive. "Thank you class, ok Jones, your parents are here." – Lets switch back to group

5A's perspective. – "Yessss, it's hometime," yelled Mina. She rushed to the door, more energetic than ever, to be received by her parents. "WHERE DO YOU THINK YOU'RE GOING MISSY?" "Errr, hometime?" "GET BACK TO YOUR SEAT THIS INSTANT!" Mina burst into tears as she picked up this direct message from Mr Sanchez. "Typical Mina," replied Oscar in an immature voice. "DO YOU WANT ME TO SHOUT TO YOU TOO OR NOT?" – He is a man of many words, and of course, many arguments. – "WILL YOU TOO STOP TALKING ABOUT ME, AUTHOR?" – Chillax man, no need to be harsh. – "I SAID, - Ok ok, you are one ferocious, - STOP TALKING ABOUT ME!" – mighty man. – Shhhhhhhhh – Oh no, he's going to explode! – "Aaaargh, his ear steam is acting like fog," shouted Figo. "I can't see," bellowed Mina. – The classroom is covered in fog.

This isn't looking good. – "Atchoo!" "Mester, are you ok," asked Garry. "Ah, ah, ATCHOO!" – Just to let you know, Mester is allergic to 'ear steam' – "I..I..I a..a..am o..o..k..ok," said Mester, his words tumbling with torture. "ATCHOOOOOOOOOOOOOO OOOOOOO!" – That one blew it - "Stop talking Anil, you just ruined the scene!" – Sorry Garry, I'm the author so I decide what happens next – "I will get you!" – You're lucky I created you Garry – "Well you've got a point but this is me and I will do what I want with myself. We're not getting anywhere with this story so better stop chit-chatting and better start typing. – But I am typing – "Just start carrying on the plot. We're not getting anywhere by just talking to each other." – You've got a point – "We're even now." - Sorry about the long talk; lets get back to the story –

Chapter 23- The end is near

Jane merrily said, "I can see!" "I can finally widen my pupils too," responded Ralph. – All now could see as the smog retreated out of the glossy window. "I can finally see," said Mr Sanchez. "Where were we?" "Hometime," replied Garry. "Oh yeah sending you grubs out of this class, no offense Mester and Jane." Mester looked at Mr Sanchez, puzzled. "Can't you see I'm sneezing?" "Oh sorry Mester, are you ok?" "I'm g..o..o..d. ATCHOOO!"

"Your mum is here Mester. "Bye Mester," spoke the class in union. "Bye class," countered Mester. "Buh bye Mesterrr," retorted Mina.

Chapter 24- The journey back

"How was your day," asked Mester's mum, in a well mannered, polite way. "I suppose it was alright until after lunch when the maths mech broke down so we had to have a substitute teacher to come in." "And who was that?" "Surprisingly, it was the head teacher." "What? I thought that the head teacher was meant to be in his office writing the report cards, especially for you."

"That's what I thought too. Guess the day turned out differently mum." "So what happened today?" "It was a mixture of different things. First the school bully Greedy Gotham comes out then the next thing, Freddy farts so badly that the cool kid smells it and goes nuts! Can you believe it? The cool kid. Out of everyone that could of picked up that faulty scent, it was the cool kid. All thanks to the stupid window."
Mester covered his mouth in shock.

"I beg your pardon Mester," shouted Mester's mum in disgust. – You might be wondering what just occurred right now. Mester never used a rude word in his life, so it would be a very big deal for him. – "I'm so sorry mum," sobbed Mester. "It's ok Mester. Mistakes happen to everyone. We're not perfect," replied Mum, neglecting what she said to Mester. His tears slowly faded away as he took a big sigh of relief. Mester carried on talking.

"After that, the school shook once Miss Elize squeaked so loud." "Why?" "Because Mina was late as predicted. "I should have known that." "Mum, my friends are here. Please can I go and talk to them?" "Sure. Anything for you." "Thanks mum, I'll be right back." Mester went to join his friends. "Did you guys have a good day," asked Mester. "I was being chased by the bully," answered Zee. "And I got tired so the bully closed on me. Luckily, I managed to escape.

Maybe a stitch from all that running." "I wouldn't want to be in your shoes. I feel bad for you Zee," stated Mester, sadly. "My house is around the bend. I should get going." "Mine's around the bend too," bluffed Zee. "Bye Zee," announced Mester. "Bye Mester," stated Zee, his voice fading into the distance. "We're home," shouted Mester's mum as she unlocked the door using her keys. – FYI, Mester's mum was talking to Mester's dad – "Ok," said Mester's dad in a deep voice. "So what would you like for supper?" Mester replied, "Can I please have fish? I stick to nutritional food." "That's my boy," replied Mester's mum in a cheerful tone. "I'll get cooking right away." – A few hours later – "That was so good! I'm stuffed," Mester babbled. "I'm glad to hear that," responded Mester's mum. Tom softly purred as he rubbed his head on Mester's leg. – Tom is a cat, if you didn't know that – "Oh Tom, you are the the cutest cat anyone could have," merrily said Mester. "Meow." "Mester, you know what time it is." "Mum, is it bedtime already?" "Yes Mester. Night night." "Goodnight." Mester walked to his bedroom with Tom following him. "Tom, doesn't time fly by so quickly?" "Meow." "Mester?" "Yes mum?" "I love you." "I love you too," replied Mester. Mester jumped into bed.

"This was a weird day, wasn't it?" "Meow." "Time to sleep Tom." Tom jumped onto Mester's bed and curled up into a ball. "Goodnight." "Meeow."

The End

Marvellous Mester encounters a series of parts that could be interesting or completely bonkers! Let us see if it goes alright or all wrong...

ANIL BUYUKADAM

Printed in Great Britain
by Amazon